40
Conversations
WITH
GOD
THAT BRING
PEACE
AND
JOY

SUSAN FRANTZ BELISLE

ISBN: 9798422735792

Cover Design: Tehsin Gull

Typesetting by: HMDpublishing

Unless otherwise noted, all Scripture quotations are taken from the Holy Bible, New International Version ® NIV. Copyright © 1973, 1978, 1984, 2011 by Biblica, Inc.™. Used by permission of Zondervan. All rights reserved worldwide. www.zondervan.com The "NIV" and "New International Version" are registered trademarks registered in the United States Patent and Trademark Office by Biblica, Inc. ™

Also used: Scriptures marked AMP are taken from the AMPLIFIED BIBLE (AMP): Scripture taken from the AMPLIFIED® BIBLE, Copyright © 1954, 1958, 1962, 1964, 1965, 1987 by the Lockman Foundation. Used by permission. (www.lockman.org)

Also used: The Holy Bible, Berean Study Bible, BSB. Copyright ©2016, 2020 by Bible Hub. Used by Permission. All Rights Reserved Worldwide.

Scriptures marked CEV are taken from the CONTEMPORARY ENGLISH VERSION (CEV): Scripture taken from the CONTEMPORARY ENGLISH VERSION copyright© 1995 by the American Bible Society. Used by permission.

Scripture quotations marked CSB are been taken from the Christian Standard Bible®, Copyright © 2017 by Holman Bible Publishers. Used by permission. Christian Standard Bible• and CSB® are federally registered trademarks of Holman Bible Publishers.

Scriptures marked ESV are taken from THE HOLY BIBLE, ENGLISH STANDARD VERSION (ESV): Scriptures taken from THE HOLY BIBLE, ENGLISH STANDARD

Scripture quotations are from The ESV® Bible (The Holy Bible, English Standard Version®), copyright © 2001 by Crossway, a publishing ministry of Good News Publishers. Used by permission. All rights reserved.

All Scripture marked with the designation "GW" is taken from GOD'S WORD®.© 1995, 2003, 2013, 2014, 2019, 2020 by God's Word to the Nations Mission Society. Used by permission.

Scriptures marked KJV are taken from the KING JAMES VERSION (KJV): KING JAMES VERSION, public domain.

Scriptures marked NASB are taken from the NEW AMERICAN STANDARD (NAS): Scripture taken from the NEW AMERICAN STANDARD BIBLE®, copyright© 1960, 1962, 1963, 1968, 1971, 1972, 1973, 1975, 1977, 1995 by The Lockman Foundation. Used by permission.

Scripture quoted by permission. Quotations designated (NET) are from the NET Bible® copyright ©1996, 2019 by Biblical Studies Press, L.L.C. http://netbible.com All rights reserved

Scriptures marked NLT are taken from the New Living Translation copyright © 1996, 2004, 2007 by Tyndale House Foundation. Used by permission of Tyndale House Foundation. Used by permission of Tyndale House Publishers Inc., Carol Stream, IL 60188. All rights reserved. New Living, NLT, and the New Living Translation logo are registered trademarks of Tyndale House Publishers.

Scriptures marked TPT are from The Passion Translation®. Copyright © 2017, 2018, by Passion & Fire Ministries, Inc. Used by permission.

Dedication

This book is lovingly dedicated to my parents, Bob and Linda Frantz. I thank God that He chose you to be my parents.

Thank you for always supporting and believing in me. I am deeply grateful for the Christian foundation that you instilled in my life and am continually inspired by your passion for Kingdom service. My life has been shaped and formed by your examples of kindness, generosity, and servanthood.

I have fond memories of the many vacations we have taken together at Kiawah Island, South Carolina. It was on our most recent visit to this beautiful island that I wrote a large portion of this book. Thank you for giving me the place, space, and freedom to do that. Your investment in Kingdom work will touch the lives of many for years to come.

I love you from the depths of my heart and treasure each day that I have you in my life.

Contents

A Thank You Gift

Thank you for choosing to read 40 Conversations That Bring Peace and Joy. In addition to this book, I'd like to give you a personally recorded video where I walk you through my 7-step outline for living a life filled with peace and joy. You may use this during your devotional or study time or just listen to it whenever convenient.

To receive your free video, visit www.SusanBelisle.com/peace-joy

Blessings in Christ,

Susan Belisle

Introduction

Have you ever felt that peace has eluded you? Have you searched for joy but could find it nowhere? This seems to be the plight of many. We understand that the Bible speaks of God's promises for peace and joy, yet it escapes many in their day-to-day living.

There is a multitude of problems that bombard us daily. The chaos of our modern-day culture fights to replace our peace and joy with anxiety and despair. However, God has promised in His Word that He will never leave us, and He will never abandon us. When we fully realize that He gives us the authority to overcome this world, we can rest in His promises and stand on the truths of His Word.

At the writing of this book, we have endured months... now heading toward years of a deadly epidemic that has wrapped its' ugly tentacles around the earth. Each one of us has been impacted in some manner by this virus. Some have been sick, some have died, and some have had a financial loss. Many have been gripped by fear and others have lost hope. Most grieve over our loss of freedom and the lives we once knew.

This epidemic has been more than an inconvenience. Restrictions, lockdowns, mandates, and business closings have taken a devastating toll on many. It has been a monster that is trying to kill, steal, and destroy everyone and everything in its' path.

The emotional turmoil to young and old alike has been countless. Some are struggling spiritually trying to make sense of what's happening in the world. Some are trying even harder to hold on to faith in God. There is a flux of emotions driven by the latest news and what's happening around us. Many are crying out, "I want my life back!" What they are saying is, "I want my joy back. I want my peace back. I want to live the life that I have always dreamed of."

Amid a crisis that should bring us together, our country is separated by political viewpoints that become more polarized and magnified with each passing day. Racial tension and division continually create conflict. There is violence, slandering, and hatred all around. Civility and respect have become a casualty of our present culture. We are divided, broken, and, seemingly have lost our way. We cry out for peace on earth and goodwill to all men, yet we continue to ride this roller coaster of emotional turmoil.

In addition to the current chaos of this world, there is a growing epidemic of drug and alcohol abuse. People's lives and families are being destroyed by addictions. Some are confused about their identity. Teenage pregnancies and fatherless homes have taken a toll on the family structure. We have removed God from our schools leaving a void in the moral fabric of our nation.

These problems are not limited to any one country or culture but extend to those throughout the world. International news outlets continually fill our homes and our minds with the problems of this world. Everywhere we turn there seems to be conflict, problems, and despair. It appears to be an endless cycle that we are trapped in. We struggle to find peace in the middle of the mess

Yet, in the midst of all *this*, Jesus is calling us to live a victorious life. He desires for us to experience an abundant life that is full of His peace and joy. But how can this be possible? Can we experience peace in our hearts and joy in our souls when there are so many challenges in life? The answer is a resounding YES!

A Biblical Perspective

In the book of Philippians, we find a powerful example of joy and passion in the life of Paul. He found himself a prisoner in Rome, but it was here that he wrote fifteen explicit references about joy. It's almost unimaginable that he could write of joy while chained to a Praetorian guard and awaiting a trial that could end his life.

In August 2019, my husband, Sam, and I visited Rome. It was an amazing experience seeing the grandeur of the Roman empire. On that trip, we visited the Mamertine Prison where Paul penned his letter to the Philippians. This is not the kind of prison that I have seen portrayed on television. It was difficult for me to imagine Paul's experience in this dark and damp prison cell. How could he write of joy in such a dismal place? Paul's life had been radically transformed by his relationship with Jesus, the gospel message, and his sense of mission. He walked with Jesus. He talked with Jesus. Paul held on to the teachings of Christ and the truth of His words even after His death and ascension to Heaven. He could no longer see, touch, or be with Jesus, but the radical impact that Jesus made on his life compelled Paul to move forward.

The Bible also speaks of situations in which God's peace prevailed despite the apparent hazards. In Matthew 8:23

– 27, Jesus demonstrated His authority over the elements when He said "peace be still." In Daniel chapter 6, the prophet Daniel continued his daily practice of prayer to his God knowing that he would be thrown into the Lion's Den. Esther, Queen of Persia, entered the King's court with quiet confidence knowing that to be rejected by the King meant death. The Hebrew children, Shadrach, Meshach, and Abednego, had peace as they were bound and thrown into a fiery furnace. Mary, as she carried Jesus in her womb, had peace in her heart after her encounter with the angel of the Lord. Steven had peace even while he was being stoned. Jesus, while He walked on this earth, had peace knowing He had come to fulfill His Father's mission.

Can We Experience Peace and Joy No Matter What?

Whether you are experiencing life on the mountain summit or the valley floor, you can be filled with God's peace and have joy overflowing. Jesus knew that there would be hard times in life.

He knew that we would experience trials and tribulation. Yet He said in John 16:33 (KJV), "These things I have spoken unto you, that in me, ye might have peace. In the world ye shall have tribulation: but be of good cheer; I have overcome the world."

Our joy is complete knowing that God has the power to do anything…anytime…anywhere. He has truly overcome the world, and He empowers us to be overcomers, as well. We do not have to live beneath our circumstances. We can live above them. We can have more mountaintop than valley experiences.

When the storm is raging around us we must keep our eyes fixed on Jesus. If we allow ourselves to look at the storm, we will be gripped by fear just like the Disciples on the Sea of Galilee. However, when we put our faith and trust in the Peace Speaker – the One who rebuked the wind and the sea (Mark 4:39), there is no reason to fear. In Matthew 14:22-33, we read of another storm that the Disciples experienced. Jesus walked on water toward the Disciples' boat and after announcing himself, called for Peter to "come." Peter stepped out of the boat and began to walk toward Jesus. As he did, he began to notice the waves instead of the Waymaker. He took his eyes off Jesus. What happened? He began to sink, and that's exactly what happens to us when we take our eyes off Jesus. God's promises are true, and He can be trusted so we must always look to Him during life's storms.

We must hold on to hope during our troubles. When we hold on to hope we hold on to Jesus, and by doing so, we hold on to our peace, and we hold on to our joy. It's a beautiful circle that runs continuously. Jesus…hope…peace…joy. It's never-ending when we keep our eyes on Jesus and not on the problems of this world. It's the "formula" to a peaceful and joyful life that so many are searching for.

Instead of looking to Jesus for the answers, people often look to themselves or others. When we put Jesus front and center, He blocks out all distractions that attempt to rob us of our peace and joy. He shields us from the enemy's attacks. He shines His beautiful light on our souls. The further we get from Jesus, the bigger our problems become. The further we get from Jesus, the harder life's battles become. The further we get from Jesus, the less peace and joy we will have.

We will have peace and joy when we remain in Jesus. To remain means to stay with Him. It means to stay close to Him and to never let go of Him. It means to tuck ourselves inside of His loving care. 1 Samuel 25:29 (NLT) says that we are safe and secure in God's treasure pouch.

Too many people step away from God when life is hard. They become disillusioned when God doesn't answer their prayers as they desire. Many are satisfied to keep Him at an arm's length's distance and only call upon Him in moments of desperation. The further away we are from God the more we see what's happening around us. The world and all its' problems become bigger, and God with all His power and majesty becomes smaller in our eyes. When we keep God close to us, He is magnified, and we will see less of the troubles around us. We will not feel and experience them as we would when we are far from Him.

The closer we get to God the less we see of our enemies. The giants shrink as God becomes bigger in our eyes, and more of God in our lives ensures more peace and joy.

God promises peace to all who follow Him. John 14:27 (NIV) says, "Peace I leave with you; my peace I give you. I do not give to you as the world gives. Do not let your hearts be troubled and do not be afraid." The New Living Translation puts it this way. "I am leaving you with a gift – peace of mind and heart. And the peace I give is a gift the world cannot give. So don't be troubled or afraid." Wow! Peace is a gift that God has given to us. When He left this earth for His heavenly home, He did not leave us without peace, and He did not leave us without hope. God gave us a roadmap for life and living when He gave us the Bible, and everything we need is found inside. It contains the "formula" for those seeking peace and joy. Where there is peace there is joy, and where there is joy there is peace. The two go hand-in-hand.

Amid all our earthly trials, God is saying that we can have peace, and we can have His unending joy.

So what's the "formula" for having peace and joy in your life?

Jesus First + Jesus Front & Center + Remain in Him =
Peace and Joy

A Guide for Using This Journal

In my first book, 40 Conversations With God That Will Change Your Life, I shared about how I began to hear the voice of God, and I outline how you can begin to hear His voice too.

As you begin your journey, I encourage you to incorporate these daily readings into your daily time with the Lord. Although this devotional is written as a 40-day journey, you may begin at day one, day forty, or skip randomly through the days. You can begin or end your quiet time with this book or use it somewhere in between. It is not intended to replace your time of worship, Bible reading, or prayer, but rather to complement it. You can also read the Word, pray, and worship while using this devotional. Lastly, you may choose to end your day by reading this devotional.

Meaningful conversation involves two people. God talks to us, and we talk to Him. I am a believer in the power of journaling so I have provided a section each day for you to talk to God. This is a place where you can respond to God about what He has spoken to you. You may even want to get a separate notebook just for this purpose since your conversations may be longer than the space provided.

God can speak to us at any time and in any way, so press in to hear His voice. Make your time with Him a priority. Pour out your heart and cry out to God. He is waiting to meet you and speak to you about all the things that matter most in your life.

Day 1

God Loves You

And may you have the power to understand, as all God's people should, how wide, how long, how high, and how deep his love is.
Ephesians 3:18 NLT

God's Conversation With Me

I love you, My precious child. You are beautiful in My sight. I hope you feel My deep love for you. It is a love that will never fade away. It is a love that endures forever. It is a love that will fill you with My peace and with My joy. Rest in knowing that My love for you cannot be broken. It cannot be taken away. Nothing will separate you from My love. My extravagant love for you will stand the test of time.

Nothing and no one can separate us. Knowing that should fill you with pure joy. If everything else in life seems to be falling apart, meditate on My love for you. That alone should lift your spirits. It should fill you with My joy. It should keep you going day after day. Meditate on My love for you. That is the remedy for heartache. It is the remedy for everything in life that hurts. Meditate on My love for you and see what I will do.

My Conversation with God

Prayer

Heavenly Father, I am so overwhelmed by Your extravagant love for me. I feel it deep within my soul. I am at peace knowing that nothing and no one can separate us or take Your love from me. My heart is filled with joy as I meditate on Your love for me. AMEN.

Day 2

God Sends His Peace

Let the peace of Christ rule in your hearts, since as members of one body you were called to peace. And be thankful.
Colossians 3:15 NIV

God's Conversation With Me

Peace, peace wonderful peace. I send it down from Heaven. This is not a peace that man can understand. It is a peace that the Father gives. I want you to have more peace in your life. I want you to remain in My peace.

This world needs more of My peace. It needs more of my joy. This world needs to put its' trust in Me. People look to too many other sources for the answers. People look to man when they should look to Me. I have everything that you need and that which you long for. Ask Me, and I will give it to you. I want to bless you. You are My precious child, and I love you.

My Conversation with God

_____

_____

_____

_____

_____

_____

_____

_____

_____

_____

_____

Prayer

Father, I desire to have more peace in my life. I don't want to experience a roller coaster of emotions based on how I feel or what is happening whether good or bad. Forgive me for the times I have looked to other people or things for answers. Help me look to You and You alone. AMEN.

Day 3

Stay Focused on Me

*You will keep in perfect peace those whose minds are steadfast,
because they trust in you. Trust in the Lord forever, for the Lord,
the Lord himself, is the Rock eternal. Isaiah 26:3-4*

God's Conversation With Me

My joy and My peace transcend all understanding. Who can understand the peace I give to you in unbearable circumstances? This can only come from Me – your Heavenly Father.

I give peace, and I give joy when you stay focused on Me. When you focus on the problems in this world you will end up in a pit of despair. You will wander. You will worry. You will find yourself in a very bad place. So always stay focused on Me, and you will always have peace and joy.

My Conversation with God

_____

_____

_____

_____

_____

_____

_____

_____

_____

_____

_____

Prayer

Lord, Help me stay focused on You and You alone. When my eyes wander so does my heart, and I succumb to worry and fear. As I keep my eyes on You, give me Your peace that passes all understanding. My heart's desire is for more of You, and more of your peace in my life. AMEN.

Day 4

God Will Take Care of Things

You will keep in perfect peace those whose minds are steadfast,
because they trust in you.
Isaiah 26:3

God's Conversation With Me

Oh, My child, I love you. This alone should bring you joy overflowing. Knowing, receiving, and understanding My love for you should flood your soul with overwhelming joy.

Why are you sad? Why do you worry? Why are you distracted by all the chaos around you? It is nothing to Me. It is nothing that I cannot handle. I am God and Creator of the universe. Do you think this is too big for Me? Do you think I can't handle your problems? I can and will take care of every one of them.

You must learn to trust Me more. You must learn to rest in Me. You must learn to put your hope in Me – not man, not the government, not a program, and not a person. Put your trust in Me. Believe in Me, and believe in My power to take care of things to completion. I will do it. I promise.

My Conversation with God

_____

_____

_____

_____

_____

_____

_____

_____

_____

_____

_____

Prayer

Heavenly Father, Thank you for Your extravagant love for me. Help me to fully trust in You no matter what is going on around me. Help me to rest in my spirit knowing that You have complete control of all things and are working them out for my good. AMEN.

Day 5

God's Peace is a Gift

A calm and peaceful and tranquil heart is life and health to the body… Proverbs 14:30 AMP

God's Conversation With Me

Let My peace permeate your soul. Let it refresh your spirit. Let it flow to every part of your being. My peace brings life to your weary body. It brings refreshment. It brings new life to you. I want you to experience the abundant life that I have destined you for. It is a life overflowing with peace, joy, and purpose.

I have much for you to do in this life, and you will accomplish it more easily when your life is full of My peace.

Don't let anyone or anything take away your peace. It is a precious gift that I have given to you. Treasure it. Store it up for when times are tough. It will help carry you through the battles of life. Nothing will affect you when you are clothed in My peace. As you remain in Me, you will remain in My peace.

My Conversation with God

_____

_____

_____

_____

_____

_____

_____

_____

_____

_____

_____

Prayer

Lord, Refresh my soul today. I long for more of You and more of Your peace and joy. I desire to experience the abundant life that You have purposed for me. I will hold tightly to Your gift of peace. I will treasure it, and cling to it when times are tough. Help me to remain in You. AMEN.

Day 6

I Give You Life

The thief comes only to steal and kill and destroy; I came so that they would have life, and have it abundantly. John 10:10 NASB

God's Conversation With Me

The enemy of your soul has tried to rob you of your joy and peace, but I have come to give you life – abundant life. The life I give supersedes all the problems of this world. It brings a continual flow of peace and joy to your life. It is a joy that cannot be stolen from you. It is a peace that passes all understanding.

My life in you brings abundant life for you. Pursue life in Me, and you will have everything you need – everything. You will have overflowing peace and joy. You will have abundance. You will have LIFE!

My Conversation with God

_____

_____

_____

_____

_____

_____

_____

_____

_____

_____

_____

Prayer

Heavenly Father, I long for the peace that You have promised me. I desire to have an abundant life. Help me to pursue You alone for in You I have everything I need. I seek You and expect to have peace and joy overflowing. AMEN.

Day 7

Choose Peace and Joy

Consider it pure joy, my brothers and sisters, whenever you face trials of many kinds, 3 because you know that the testing of your faith produces perseverance. Let perseverance finish its work so that you may be mature and complete, not lacking anything.
James 1:2-4

God's Conversation With Me

Peace and joy I will give you today. I want you to live in a perpetual state of peace and joy. This is not just something that I give you when life is easy. Rather, it is something that I give in the toughest of times.

My peace and My joy are not dependent upon the circumstances around you. They are not dependent upon how life is treating you. They are not dependent upon whether you are winning or losing. My peace and My joy supersede all hardships and all the trials of your life.

You can have My peace and My joy no matter what. You must fight for it. You must be intentional about choosing it every day. I will give it to you. Just ask.

My Conversation with God

_____

_____

_____

_____

_____

_____

_____

_____

_____

_____

_____

_____

Prayer

Heavenly Father, Today I receive the peace and joy that You freely give to me. No matter what is happening in my life I know that it is mine for the taking. So today I am asking You to give me an extra measure of Your peace and Your joy. AMEN.

Day 8

Wonderful Peace God Gives

The Lord gives strength to his people; the Lord blesses his people with peace. Psalm 29:11

God's Conversation With Me

Peace, peace wonderful peace I give to you. No one can fill your life with peace as I can. It is a beautiful gift that I give to you. Treasure this gift. Care for this gift. Don't neglect it. Don't take it for granted. It is precious.

I give you sweet peace to soothe your soul when life is hard. When you feel that the world is coming against you reach deep inside yourself for My peace. I have deposited a reservoir of My peace inside you. Don't allow the cares of this world to squelch it. Don't allow My peace to be suppressed. Don't allow it to fade away. It will be with you for a lifetime if you will stay close to Me. If you will passionately pursue Me. I will continue to fill you with My peace. It will envelop your life like a warm blanket on a cold day. You will be at peace in your life when you pursue Me above all things. Remain in My peace.

My Conversation with God

Prayer

Lord, I need Your peace today. My heart and my mind often feel restless because I allow too many things to bother me. My joy is often squelched because I allow the cares of this world to weigh me down. Help me to pursue You more so that I live a life of continual peace. AMEN.

Day 9

God's Provision is Abundant

Do it again! Those Yahweh has set free will return to Zion and come celebrating with songs of joy! They will be crowned with never-ending joy! Gladness and joy will overwhelm them; despair and depression will disappear! Isaiah 51:11 TPT

God's Conversation With Me

I am releasing My joy inside of you. A joy that cannot be contained. A joy that will overflow from your life. A joy that is unspeakable and full of mercy and grace.

Joy I give to you, and peace I give to you. No man can give you the joy that comes from Me. No circumstances and no events can give you what I can give you. I have an abundance of a provision in My storehouse. It is all there for you.

What do you want? What do you need? I will give it to you if you will just ask Me. Seek Me, and you will find everything you need in this life.

My Conversation with God

_____

_____

_____

_____

_____

_____

_____

_____

_____

_____

_____

_____

Prayer

Lord Jesus, I am excited about the joy that is rising within me. I pray that it overflows from my life into the lives of others. Forgive me for the times I've tried to find joy in other places for only You can give that to me. Today, I receive Your abundance of joy. AMEN.

Day 10

Walk In God's Way

Stay alert! Watch out for your great enemy, the devil. He prowls around like a roaring lion, looking for someone to devour.
1 Peter 5:8 NLT

God's Conversation With Me

My way is the way of life – abundant life. A life without worry and a life without stress. I freely give you My peace and My joy. Nothing and no one can take this from you. You, however, can give it away. You can squander it. You can allow it to be stolen from you.

The thief – the enemy of your soul – wants to steal your joy. He wants to defeat you. He wants to crush you. But if you will remain in Me and remain in My Word, I will envelop you with My love, and I will give you peace.

Always stay close to Me – close to My Heart, and I will give you peace. I will give you joy. I will give you everything you need in this life.

My Conversation with God

Prayer

Lord, Help me to stay alert so that the enemy cannot steal my joy. I desire to have an abundant life that is free of worry and free of stress. I commit to staying close to You always. Fill me with Your peace and joy overflowing. AMEN.

Day 11

Stay Connected to the Vine

I am the vine; you are the branches. If you remain in me and I in you, you will bear much fruit; apart from me you can do nothing.
John 15:5

God's Conversation With Me

Joy…joy…joy…down in your soul. My deep and abiding joy I give to you. This is not the kind of joy you sing about at Christmas, but rather, it is a joy that permeates your being no matter what is happening in your life. It's the kind of joy that puts a permanent smile on your face. It's a joy that puts a sparkle in your eyes. It is My joy, and it is straight from Heaven. It's a joy that makes you laugh for no reason at all. This is My joy, and I impart it to you freely.

Just stay connected to My vine, and you will have continual joy. Your joy will produce everlasting peace. My joy brings peace, and My peace brings joy. Have a JOYFUL day in Me

My Conversation with God

Prayer

Lord, I receive your joy deep down inside my soul. Thank you for Your gift of joy that You impart to me freely. Help me to stay connected to You so that my joy is unending. I desire Your peace that produces everlasting joy. AMEN.

Day 12

Receive God's Peace Today

Then you will experience God's peace, which exceeds anything we understand. His peace will guard your hearts and minds as you live in Christ Jesus. Philippians 4:7 NLT

God's Conversation With Me

Feel My peace flowing over you today. I know that life feels stressful right now. I know that it seems the world is falling apart, but know that I am with you. I am near, and I will give you peace. It is a supernatural peace that you cannot begin to comprehend.

When it feels that everything around you is falling apart reach for My peace. It will carry you through the toughest of times. It will take you to My secret place where we will commune together.

In My presence, you will find My peace. It surpasses anything this world has to offer. The world only offers you substitutes for My true peace. What the world offers pales in comparison to My ever-abiding peace. It is real, and I will give you all the peace you need for your life right now. I will give you what you need in the future. I will always give you everything you need. Just ask and then receive.

My Conversation with God

_____

_____

_____

_____

_____

_____

_____

_____

_____

_____

_____

Prayer

Lord, I long to be in Your presence and experience the fullness of Your peace. I pray that it would flow over me washing away my stress, burdens, and worries. Forgive me for looking to other people and things for the peace that only You can give. Today, I receive your peace. AMEN.

Day 13

God's Joy and Peace Sustain You

The Lord gives strength to his people; the Lord blesses his people with peace. Psalm 29:11

God's Conversation With Me

I want you to have My joy overflowing. I want you to have My peace. My joy and My peace will sustain you during the trials of life. They never run out because I keep giving them to you freely. I love to fill you with My joy because I love you My child, and I want you to experience a joy-filled life. I want you to have a life that is permeated by My peace.

The world is shaking. It is unsettled. There is hardship and trouble all around, but I am your source of peace. You do not need to be concerned. If you will keep your eyes fixed on Me, you will have the joy and peace that I have promised you. You will have everything that you need and so much more. Remain in Me, and you will remain in My peace. Remain in Me, and you will have joy overflowing.

My Conversation with God

_____

_____

_____

_____

_____

_____

_____

_____

_____

_____

Prayer

God, Thank you for being my source of peace and joy. Thank you for the strength that You give me in all circumstances. I look to You for my peace and find my joy in You alone. I will trust You with every situation that concerns me, and find rest in You. AMEN.

Day 14

Just Do Your Job

Just as the body is dead without breath, so also faith is dead without good works. James 2:26 NLT

God's Conversation With Me

Joy, My child, I want you to have more joy in your life. Why do you worry, and why do you fret about the things of this world? They are of no concern to you. I am God, and I am in control of all things. Let Me do My job, and you do yours. Your job is to remain in Me. Your job is to be My disciple. Your job is to love Me, and love people.

People need your love, and they need your joy. They need your peace, and they need your happiness. They don't need your sorrow, and your worry, and your doubt. They need to see your faith in action, and your faith will produce good works that will help change this world. Let's change this world together. I'll lead, and you follow. Together we will do it.

My Conversation with God

Prayer

God, Fill me with Your love, joy, and peace. I want to be a light that shines pointing others to You. I pray that people see My good works done in Your name and for Your glory. I pray that hearts and lives are changed because of Your joy inside of me. AMEN.

Day 15

God Has Overcome The World

I have told you these things, so that in me you may have peace. In this world you will have trouble. But take heart! I have overcome the world. John 16:33

God's Conversation With Me

My peace and My joy I give to you. It does not come from the things of this world. It comes directly from Me – a download from Heaven.

This world is perplexing. It is ridden with problems. Everywhere you look there is trouble, but take heart for I have overcome the things of this world. My peace can and will prevail on this earth. Look to Me daily as your source of peace, and I will also instill My joy deep inside your soul.

Do not look at the problems all around you. Look to Me for I have all the answers to your problems. When you look to Me I will not only give you the answers, but I will give you peace – deep and abiding peace in your soul. My peace I give to you if you will just receive it, My child. Receive My peace, and you will also have My joy.

My Conversation with God

Prayer

Heavenly Father, It seems that there are troubles all around me. Help me to look to You always knowing that You have overcome and are in control of all things. I put my trust and hope in You. You are my source of peace and joy. AMEN.

Day 16

Take Time to Laugh

Now may God, the fountain of hope, fill you to overflowing with uncontainable joy and perfect peace as you trust in him. And may the power of the Holy Spirit continually surround your life with his super-abundance until you radiate with hope! Romans 15:13 TPT

God's Conversation With Me

Take some time to laugh today. I want your laughter to permeate this earth. You laugh because you have My joy inside of you. Let your laughter reflect My joy. My joy is like sunshine on this earth. My light is everywhere. It brings joy, hope, and peace.

My people are worn out for lack of hope. I have come to give you hope. I have come to give you peace, and I have come to give you joy. Don't allow the problems of this world to weigh you down for I have come to give you life – abundant life.

Keep your eyes on Me, and not on the things of this world. If you will do this, you will have a perpetual stream of peace and joy enveloping your life.

My Conversation with God

_____

_____

_____

_____

_____

_____

_____

_____

_____

_____

Prayer

God, Help me to laugh more because of Your joy inside of me. I want to live an abundant life that can only come from You. Help me to keep my eyes on You and not on the things of this world. As I do, I trust that You will fill my life with overflowing peace and joy. AMEN.

Day 17

Let God's Joy Fill You Up

For You make him most blessed [and a blessing] forever; You make him joyful with the joy of Your Presence.
Psalm 16:11 AMP

God's Conversation With Me

Joy! I want you to be full of My joy. It is a joy that never runs dry. It never runs out. My joy can always be with you no matter what is happening in your life.

My joy is not contingent upon everything going well for you. It is not only there during the good times, but also in the bad. This is the joy that I want you to have. Joy overflowing in every circumstance of life. Joy. My joy I freely give to you. Reach out and embrace it. Carry it with you everywhere you go. Proudly display My joy. Point people to Me when they ask about the joy that fills your life to overflowing. They can have it too if they will look to Me as their source. If they will embrace Me as their Savior, their joy will never run out. Joy – My joy – I give to you freely.

My Conversation with God

Prayer

God, I want to be full of Your joy. Freely you give it, and freely I receive it. I want Your joy to be overflowing in my life regardless of what is happening around me. I want to share Your joy with others and point people to You – the true giver of joy. AMEN.

Day 18

The Devil is Defeated

The God of peace will soon crush Satan under your feet. The grace of our Lord Jesus be with you. Romans 16:20

God's Conversation With Me

The Devil is defeated. He will no longer steal your peace and steal your joy. I defeated him on the cross when I died for your sins.

No more wasting time worrying about this, and worrying about that. No more wondering how things are going to work out. No more fretting. It is finished – all finished. It was completed on the cross. Do not pick this up and carry it with you. It is not your burden to carry. When you try to carry things you are weighed down in your spirit. You become sad and oppressed. But when you let Me carry the burdens of your life, all is well. Your load is easy and your burden is light. Take My yoke and not your own, and you will remain in My peace.

You will be filled with joy overflowing joy that no man can give you – only Me. So rest in My peace and rest in My joy today.

My Conversation with God

_____

_____

_____

_____

_____

_____

_____

_____

_____

_____

Prayer

God, Thank you that you defeated the Devil through Your death on the cross. Help me not pick up the load and try to carry it on my own. Help me to let go of my worries and concerns. Today, I put my trust in You, and rest in your peace and love. AMEN.

Day 19

Discover

God's Mysteries

He replied, "The knowledge of the mysteries of the kingdom of heaven has been given to you, but not to them." Matthew 13:11

God's Conversation With Me

I will speak to you and tell you great mysteries that you do not know. Some things are hidden from man, but I have the key to unlock those mysteries. You think that you have figured this out, but you have not. Deep inside these mysteries are rivers of joy. Rivers flowing near and far. Rivers that flow freely at My beck and call.

I will unlock the mysteries for you. I will take you deeper into My ever-abiding love for you. The deeper you go the more you will experience My love and the more you will experience My joy.

Deep and wide we will go together experiencing this wonderful life I have given you. It will be full of My joy. It will be full of My treasures. It will be full of My riches. It will be everything you could dream of or imagine. Go deeper in Me, and you will find it all.

My Conversation with God

Prayer

Heavenly Father, Unlock Your mysteries to me. I desire to have Your rivers of joy flow freely in my life. I long for greater intimacy with You, and to experience Your love to the fullest. The life You have given me is a gift that I will treasure. Fill me with Your joy beyond measure. AMEN.

Day 20

Ask and Receive Today

Until now you have not asked for anything in my name. Ask and you will receive, and your joy will be complete. John 16:24

God's Conversation With Me

Peace and joy! It is yours for the taking. It's not hard. Just reach out and grab them. I give them freely to you, and freely you should receive. Receive them right now. Hold out your hands, and I will give them to you.

Do you see the joy and peace you have by simply receiving? I will give you everything you need, but you must receive it – all of it. Hold out your hands and fully embrace the wonderful life I want to give you. Take it. It's yours.

I have destined you for greatness so don't hold back on receiving. Why do you hesitate? Are you afraid of My goodness? Why? I only give good gifts to My children. Do not allow your fear to hold you back. Your fear will rob you of My peace and joy, and that's exactly what the enemy wants. He wants you crippled and joyless. He wants your life to be in turmoil, but I have come to give you abundant life. Receive it now.

My Conversation with God

_____

_____

_____

_____

_____

_____

_____

_____

_____

_____

_____

Prayer

Heavenly Father, Thank you that You freely give to all who will ask and receive. Today, I open up my hands and stretch them toward You. Place within my hands the peace and joy that You desire to give me. I receive these and every good gift that You have for me. AMEN.

Day 21

God is in Control

The Lord reigns, He is clothed with majesty; The Lord has clothed and girded Himself with strength; Indeed, the world is firmly established, it will not be moved. Psalm 93:1

God's Conversation With Me

Stronger and stronger you will become. You will fly high above the cares and problems of this world. They are nothing to Me. I rule and I reign over all the earth. I am in control, and it's not over until I say it's over. Things are not always as they seem. I am behind the scenes working My plan so there is no need to fret and fear.

You can walk in My joy and My peace when things seem uncertain. You can walk in My joy and peace when you don't understand. You can walk in My joy, and you can walk in My peace when everything in life seems to be falling apart. Know that it is not because I am in control. You can count on that. You can trust Me always. So rest in My peace today, and embrace My joy. I am with you, and I love you, My child.

My Conversation with God

Prayer

Heavenly Father, I am so thankful that You rule and reign over this earth. Help me to trust You even when I don't see the answer. I desire to walk in Your peace and Your joy. Teach me to trust You no matter how things appear. I choose to rest in Your peace today. AMEN.

Day 22

Let God's Peace Permeate Your Life

Peace I leave you, My peace I give you; not as the world gives, do I give to you. Do not let your hearts be troubled, nor fearful.
John 14:27 NASB

God's Conversation With Me

I want your life to be full of joy. I want peace to permeate every fiber of your being. I want this to be "who" you are. Peace should not be something that you have to strive for. You should be at peace because you have Me in your life.

Why do you allow people and things to rob you of your peace? This should not be. Those things should not be greater in you than My peace. My peace is powerful. It can transform your thinking and your life. My peace brings joy to your soul. It puts a pep in your step. My peace helps you walk in confidence with no fear of what lies ahead. There is no need to fear because I am with you, and I have given you My peace. Embrace my peace. Guard it like a valuable treasure. Carry My peace with you wherever you go.

My Conversation with God

Prayer

Heavenly Father, I long for more of You and the peace that only You can give. I want Your peace to fill me up to overflowing. Let Your peace be greater in me than anything else. I embrace Your peace today and will treasure it always. AMEN.

Day 23

Experience God's Extravagant Joy

You have given me greater joy than those who have abundant harvests of grain and new wine.
Psalm 4:7 NLT

God's Conversation With Me

Joy...joy...joy! I am releasing My joy in you. It is a joy that will overwhelm your soul. It is an extravagant joy. It is a joy that no man can take away.

I am infusing My joy deep within your soul. It will permeate every fiber of your being. It is a joy that will carry you through the hardest of times. If you will keep your eyes fixed on Me, and not on the things of this world, you will have a constant and continual flow of My joy in your life.

No man can give you this joy. It only comes from your Father in Heaven. Flowing down from Heaven like a river is pure unadulterated JOY. It is a beautiful river of joy flowing straight into your soul. Receive My joy today.

My Conversation with God

_____
_____
_____
_____
_____
_____
_____
_____
_____
_____
_____

Prayer

God, I receive today the joy that only You can give. I am excited about what You are doing in my life as you release Your joy to me. I long to experience Your unending and overflowing joy. Let it permeate every fiber of my being and invade my soul. AMEN.

Day 24

God is All You Need

In Heaven I have only you, and on this earth you are all I want.
Psalm 73:25 CEV

God's Conversation With Me

Peace and joy. I want your life to be full of these. This world will give you hardship, struggle, and pain, but I have come so that you can have an abundant life – a life that is full of peace and full of joy.

Why do you let the cares of this world rob you of your peace? This should not be. You have Me in your life. What else do you need? Who else can help you besides Me? Who can solve the problems of this world? No man or woman. Not the government. Not earthly rulers. Nothing and no one can do what only I can do so stop looking to other sources for your joy and your peace. They only give false promises.

Look to Me completely for all that you need. When you do you will remain in My peace. You will not struggle, and you will not worry. You will live in peace.

My Conversation with God

_____

_____

_____

_____

_____

_____

_____

_____

_____

_____

_____

Prayer

Lord, It is You and You alone that I desire in my life. Only You can solve the problems of this world. Help me to always look to You for the answers that I seek. I will keep my eyes on You knowing that You provide everything I need. You are my peace and my joy. AMEN.

Day 25

God is The Source of Your Joy

The hope of the righteous [those of honorable character and integrity] is joy...Proverbs 10:28 AMP

God's Conversation With Me

Yes! My joy swells up within you. It is like a fountain overflowing from deep within your soul. It is gushing out from deep within. Joy overflowing. I have given you joy. My joy cannot be taken away from you. It is a joy that withstands the test of time. It is a joy that permeates for all to see.

People will begin to ask you how you have so much joy in your life. You will point them to Me always. I am the source of all your joy. I am the great Joy-giver.

Joy...joy...joy. Fill your life with My joy. Never let your joy be snuffed out. Never let it be taken away from you. In all things and all circumstances, you can have My ever-abiding joy. It is yours for the asking so just ask Me. I will give you joy.

My Conversation with God

Prayer

Lord, I am asking You today for more of Your joy. I want others to see Your joy overflowing in my life. I want it to permeate to all those around me. I promise that no one and nothing will take Your joy from me. I will carry Your joy with me throughout the rest of my life. AMEN.

Day 26

Live Life to The Fullest

You will live in joy and peace. The mountains and hills will burst into song, and the trees of the field will clap their hands.
Isaiah 55:12 NLT

God's Conversation With Me

Peace. Let My peace flow over you like a gentle stream. Let My peace bring refreshment to your soul. Let it lift you and strengthen you. Let My peace bring joy to your soul. My peace I give to you freely. It is a gift from Me. Because of My extravagant love for you.

I have provided everything you need through My death on the cross. My death not only ensured your eternal salvation but also provided for an abundant life in Me. I want you to live life to the fullest. I don't want you to be bogged down by the cares of this world. This only results in the death of your peace, and eventually a life that is void of "life."

Guard your mind and guard your soul against the peace robbers. Stay focused on Me, and I will keep you in My perfect peace. I will fill your life with joy overflowing.

My Conversation with God

_____

_____

_____

_____

_____

_____

_____

_____

_____

_____

_____

_____

Prayer

Lord, Thank you for the peace that You give so freely. It is a gift from Heaven above. I desire to live life to the fullest. Help me not get bogged down by cares and concerns that only steal my peace. Guard and protect my mind from anything that would steal my peace and joy. AMEN.

Day 27

Your Heart Will Rejoice

So you also have sorrow now. But I will see you again. Your hearts will rejoice, and no one will take away your joy from you.
John 16:22 CSB

God's Conversation With Me

I have come today to give you My peace. Your heart has been heavy. You have been sorrowful at times. I want you to break free from this today. I want you to walk in peace, and I want your joy to be explosive...overflowing for all to see.

When they ask you the source of your joy point them to Me – the Author of your faith. The One who supplies you with everything that you need and so much more.

I love to bless you, and the greatest gift that I can give you today is My joy. It is joy unspeakable, and it is truly amazing because it comes from Me.

Now go and walk in My peace and My joy today. Display it for all to see.

My Conversation with God

Prayer

Jesus, At times my heart has been so heavy. Thank you for breaking me free from my sorrow. I want to point others to You so they can also know the One who gives joy. Thank you for Your gift of joy. I will cherish it and share it wherever I go. AMEN.

Day 28

Be a Light in The Storm

God is our refuge and strength, a very present help in trouble.
Psalm 46:1 ESV

God's Conversation With Me

I am filling you with My joy. It is a supernatural joy that no one can take away from you. My joy is everlasting. It does not diminish when hard times come your way. It stands strong and helps you weather the storms of life.

When the storms come against you My joy will rise ever stronger within you. You will be a beacon of light to all those around you. You will point them to Me – the source of your joy. They will glow from within as they are enveloped with My joy. They will be at peace when they find their rest in Me. Joy and peace are what I want for everyone, and everyone can have them. Just reach out to Me the giver of joy and peace. I am the source to fill you up.

My Conversation with God

Prayer

God, You are my refuge in the storms of life. Let Your joy rise even stronger within me when the winds blow and the waves try to crush me. I pray that I would be a light for all to see as Your light and Your love and Your joy shines forth from me. AMEN.

Day 29

God's Presence Brings Peace and Joy

You make known to me the path of life; you will fill me with joy in your presence, with eternal pleasures at your right hand.
Psalm 16:11

God's Conversation With Me

Peace and joy My child. That's what I will give you today. It is free, and it is yours for the asking. All you have to do is ask Me, and reach out your hands to receive it.

I love to give gifts to My children. I love to bless them, and I want to bless you today with My peace and joy. I give it to you freely so simply receive it. Receive it as you would a priceless gift. Treasure it. Hold it tight. Never let it go. Never allow the enemy of your soul to steal it from you.

If you will take the time to be in My presence, your peace and your joy will never run out. It will never diminish. It will never fade away. So stay close to Me always. Hear My heartbeat for you. Feel My love. I love you, My precious child. Never forget that.

My Conversation with God

Prayer

Heavenly Father, Thank you for the gift of peace and joy that You so freely give. I receive it today. I will hold it tight and not allow the enemy to steal it from me. I long to be in Your presence where I can experience the fullness of Your joy. I love you. AMEN.

Day 30

Seek God

Boast in his holy name; let the hearts of those who seek the LORD rejoice. 1 Chron. 16:10 CSB

God's Conversation With Me

I am filling you with My peace. Let it wash over you and invade your soul deep within. My peace is like none other. It cannot be purchased. It cannot be manufactured. It cannot be conjured up. It can only be found in Me alone.

When you seek Me you will also find My peace. That is the key to walking in My peace – seek Me. You won't find it any other way but through Me. The world offers you many remedies, but I am the only true source of your peace.

You will find My peace when you chase after Me…when you get close to Me. The closer we become the more peace you will have. You can walk in My peace continually if you will walk close to Me always. I guarantee that! Stay close to Me, and you will stay in My peace.

My Conversation with God

_____

_____

_____

_____

_____

_____

_____

_____

_____

_____

_____

Prayer

Lord, I long for more of Your peace in my life. At times, I have tried to find Your peace in other places, but I know that it can only be found in You. Help me to stay close to You so that I can continually walk in Your peace. Today, I take Your hand and fully experience Your peace. AMEN.

Day 31

God is Doing Something New

Look, I am about to do something new; even now it is coming. Do you see it? Indeed, I will make a way in the wilderness, rivers in the desert. Isaiah 43:19 CSB

God's Conversation With Me

It is a beautiful day for I am with you. I have come to fulfill all your dreams. I have come to give you peace and joy. I have come to be all that you need in your life. I have come to restore your joy.

Things in the past are no longer. It is a new day. There are new possibilities. There are new treasures to discover. There are new mountains to climb. We will do this together. It will be a grand adventure – just Me and you.

I will fill you with so much joy that you won't be able to contain it. It will overflow from your life and infect all those around you. Your joy will be contagious spreading to all those around you. When they ask about the source of your joy always point them to Me. I am the joy-giver, and I give it freely to all those who ask.

My Conversation with God

Prayer

God, Thank you for fulfilling all my dreams. I am excited about the adventures that lie ahead. Fill me with Your over-flowing joy that will be contagious to all those around me. I promise to always point people to You – the giver of all my joy. AMEN.

Day 32

You are Not Alone

I will never, never let go your hand: I will never never forsake you.
Hebrews 13:5 WNT

God's Conversation With Me

This world is in such desperate need of My peace. There are troubles all around, but I am near. Call out to Me when you feel desperate. Call out to Me when it seems there is no hope. All you have to do is call, and I will be right there to rescue you.

I will never leave you alone to fight this battle on your own. I will always come alongside you and strengthen you with My power. I will infuse you with My Holy Spirit.

You will be empowered to do all things, and you will do it with peace and joy in your heart. My peace I give to you in all situations. Just call out to Me if you are afraid. Call out to Me if you are weary. Call out to Me, and I will give you strength. I am here. Just call.

My Conversation with God

Prayer

God, Although the battles seem to rage around me, I know that You are always with me. You will protect me. You will stand beside me and fight the battles for me. I call out to You for help today. I feel so safe in Your care, and at peace when I am in Your presence. AMEN.

Day 33

Remain in God

Let what you heard from the beginning abide in you. If what you heard from the beginning abides in you, then you too will abide in the Son and in the Father. 1 John 2:24 ESV

God's Conversation With Me

I am giving you My peace. Freely I give it to you. Embrace My peace. Wrap it around you like a warm blanket on a cold winter day. Let My peace bring warmth to your soul. Let My peace encourage you when you feel discouraged. Let it lift your spirits. My peace will always be with you if you will remain in Me.

Stay close to Me always, and I will give you everything you need including My peace. I will give you joy unspeakable. Immeasurable joy you will have if you remain in Me. If you remain in Me, I will remain in you. I will invade every aspect of your life. I will give you everything you need to live an abundant life full of My peace and My joy. So remain in Me always.

My Conversation with God

Prayer

Lord, I long to abide in You and feel Your peace and presence surrounding me. Come into my life and take control. Invade every part of me. Fill me with Your joy. Give me the abundant life that You have promised. I love You, and promise to remain in You. AMEN.

Day 34

Travel God's Path

In all your ways know and acknowledge and recognize Him, And He will make your paths straight and smooth [removing obstacles that block your way]. Proverbs 3:6 AMP

God's Conversation With Me

Ride on the waves of My joy. Let it take you to places full of fun and adventure.

When you travel the path that I have set before you, there will always be joy in your heart. You will have a pep in your step when you follow Me and My plan for you. Do not wrestle against Me or you will have sorrow and struggle. Traveling down My path and following Me will always be your source of joy.

So stay close to Me. Learn from Me, and listen to Me. I will take you on adventures that you never imagined. We will go to far-away places if only in your dreams. Remain in Me, and you will remain in My joy. I promise.

My Conversation with God

_____

_____

_____

_____

_____

_____

_____

_____

_____

_____

_____

Prayer

God, I am so excited about the adventure we are taking together. I am hopeful about the future that you have planned for me. Help me to stay close to you and to obey. I will walk on the path you have set before me so that I will continually be filled with Your joy. AMEN.

Day 35

Wrap Yourself in God's Peace

Casting all your care upon him; for he cares for you.
1 Peter 5:7 KJV

God's Conversation With Me

My peace flows over you like a gentle breeze on a warm summer day. My peace is all that you need, and I freely give it to you. Allow yourself to be wrapped in My peace. Don't be distracted by the things around you for they only steal your peace.

The cares of this world will slowly wash away your peace. It will fade away and eventually disappear altogether. I want you to have peace that is with you always, but you must keep your eyes on Me always. This is how you sustain your peace.

When you put your eyes on other people and other things you will not live a life of peace. You will live in constant turmoil and continue to look to other sources for the peace that only I can give. So it's very simple. Keep your eyes fixed on Me!

My Conversation with God

Prayer

Heavenly Father, I give you all my cares and burdens. Wrap me in Your peace and wrap me in Your love. I long to sense Your presence in my life. Help me to keep my eyes on You rather than on people and problems. I look to You alone to be the source of my peace. AMEN.

Day 36

Spread God's Joy

The people ransomed by the LORD will return. They will come to Zion singing with joy. Everlasting happiness will be on their heads [as a crown]. They will be glad and joyful. They will have no sorrow or grief.
Isaiah 35:10 GW

God's Conversation With Me

I love you, My child. You are so special to Me. I want to fill you with My joy overflowing. I want it to spill over like a beautiful water fountain. I want it to be something majestic for people to see and admire. I want it to be contagious flowing from you to others.

I want your joy to be breathtaking for all to see. My joy in you is a beautiful sight to behold. It is a precious treasure to possess. Hold on to it tightly, but also lavish it freely on others. Hold on, but let go.

Freely I have given this to you so freely you should share it with others. Your joy can bring peace and help change this world. The more joy you give away the more joy that I will give you. So spread My joy today wherever you go.

My Conversation with God

Prayer

Lord, I want Your joy to flood my soul and spillover for all to feel and see. May it flow like a beautiful river touching all those around me. I pray that Your joy in me points people to You. May it bring the glory and honor You are worthy of. I promise to spread Your joy today. AMEN.

Day 37

God Gives Peace in All Circumstances

Now may the Lord of peace Himself grant you His peace at all times and in every way [that peace and spiritual well-being that comes to those who walk with Him, regardless of life's circumstances]. The Lord be with you all.
2 Thessalonians 3:16 AMP

God's Conversation With Me

Peace. I want you to have peace always. My peace can flow endlessly in your life. You don't have to wrestle and struggle because I give you My peace.

My peace transcends every bad thing that you experience. My peace goes with you even into the dark places. Even when you are in a pit of despair My peace can be with you. Ask Me to fill you with My peace when you are sad ask Me for My peace when you are troubled, and ask Me for My peace when you can't sleep at night.

I want My peace to envelop and surround you always. It is supernatural. No man can understand how you can have peace in the midst of turmoil. Only I can do this. So stay close to Me. Stay in My presence, and you will stay in My peace.

My Conversation with God

Prayer

Jesus, I am amazed by the peace that You give me. Let it flow endlessly in my life. I pray that it never leaves me even during the darkest of times. Surround me with Your peace always. Wrap me in Your peace and tuck me in Your presence today. I long for more of You. AMEN.

Day 38

Stay in God's Presence

In Him and through faith in Him we may enter God's presence
with boldness and confidence. Ephesians 3:12 BSB

God's Conversation With Me

I want you to have more joy in your life. This life you live is not meant to always be hard. It is not meant to weigh you down, and keep you from the abundant life I have planned for you. When you focus too much on the cares of this world you lose your joy, and you have to go searching for it again. You should not have to search for My joy. I give it to you freely, but you must stay in My presence to stay in My joy.

Stay in My presence always, and you will always have joy. I want your joy to be something that you proudly wear. Wear it like a badge of honor that I have bestowed upon you. Wear it proudly for all to see. When they ask about your joy point them to Me always. I am and will always be your true source of joy.

My Conversation with God

Prayer

Lord, I will run to You, and run into Your presence. I long to be there every day. In Your presence, I am shielded from the hard places in life, and I can live in Your abundance. Today, I embrace Your joy. Thank you for being my true source of joy. AMEN.

Day 39

God's Plan

is Wonderful

For I know what I have planned for you,' says the LORD. 'I have plans to prosper you, not to harm you. I have plans to give you a future filled with hope. Jeremiah 29:11 NET

God's Conversation With Me

I am filling you with My joy today. Do you feel it rising within you? Let it fill you to overflowing. My joy is all you need to experience abundant life. I want you to have a life that is full of Me and full of My goodness. It is a wonderful life that I have planned for you, and you can experience this no matter what is going on around you.

Do not allow yourself to be distracted by the cares of this world. Keep your eyes on Me – the Joy-giver. My joy transcends all earthly struggles. It can be ever-present even in the storms of life.

My joy is free for the taking. Just ask Me, and I will give you joy. When you are lacking joy ask Me to fill you up. My source is endless. Just ask, and I will give you My joy overflowing in your life.

My Conversation with God

_____

_____

_____

_____

_____

_____

_____

_____

_____

_____

Prayer

Heavenly Father, I'm so grateful that I can experience a wonderful life even during the storms. You always carry me through to the other side. Your joy lifts me, and I ask for Your overflowing joy today. I am excited about and embrace the future You have planned for me. AMEN.

Day 40

Guard Your Peace

Guard your heart above all else, for it determines the course of your life. Proverbs 4:23 NLT

God's Conversation With Me

Joy and peace I give to you. If you truly want it, it is yours. Yours for the keeping. No one can take it away. Only you can give it. Guard it with all your heart and with all your life. Don't let anyone steal it from you. It is precious, and you must not allow it to be taken from you.

You can allow yourself to give it away or you can allow it to be taken away, but I will help you maintain your peace and joy. It is a precious gift from Me, and you must treat it as such. Do not squander it. Do not treat it lightly. It is a treasure from above. You don't have to go searching for this treasure. I freely place it in your hands. Hold on to it. It will bring life to your life. It will bring sweetness to your soul. It will carry you through the hard times. My peace and joy I give to you today.

My Conversation with God

Prayer

Lord, I thank You for the peace and joy that You freely give to me. I receive them today. I will treat these as precious gifts and treasure them every day. I commit that no person or situation will rob me of Your peace and joy. I will not give it away. Today, I choose LIFE. AMEN.

Conclusion

I've always been in awe of people who are filled with the joy of Christ while living in the hardest of circumstances. It's truly amazing to witness someone who has endured tremendous hardship or abuse in life yet glows with the joy of the Lord. A few years ago, I heard a woman named Myriam speak of the beatings and other abuse she had endured as a result of her profession of faith in Christ. It was truly amazing to see the smile on her face and the peace and joy in her heart as she shared about her work for God. Only a loving God can truly transform a life and restore a person's joy after heartache or devastation such as this. Only the Prince of Peace can envelop a person with peace amid a storm. Only God our Healer can bring wholeness to a heart and life that are broken.

I wish I could say that I have always maintained my peace and joy as I have weathered the storms of life. When I began writing this book, I thought that my conversations with God were primarily for the readers. However, during this journey, I realized that God was speaking to me too. I have experienced tests from every side, and I struggled to maintain my peace as I struggled to share this message. It's been a wrestling match between my mind, will, and emotions. At times, I have allowed this to stifle my joy.

Even during the writing of this book, I've been challenged by many different circumstances that have battered my soul. I have experienced every gamut of emotions as I have grieved for the losses of others, felt disappointment, experienced sickness, been overtaken by sadness, and been hit from every side by trouble and hardship. I have gone from mountaintop-like emotions to feeling as if I was in a pit that I could not climb out of. I believe that God has allowed me to experience those feelings so that I could share with a greater depth of understanding and compassion.

Although I have experienced various hardships in life, I cannot honestly say that I have always learned the lessons that God intended for me. I have often failed, but our gracious and loving God continues to transform my life as I surrender my desires to Him and accept His will rather than mine. He can do the same for you if you will just surrender. Surrender means that we trust God fully. It means that we give Him control and turn all matters over to Him. More than just about anything, surrender brings peace and joy. And as we surrender, God is teaching us lifelong lessons and forming us into His likeness. Even if we feel that we are sinking deeper, He is taking us higher.

What does God want to teach us when we are in the midst of life's storms?

He wants to teach us to trust in Him. He wants to teach us to lean on Him. He wants to teach us to rest in Him. He wants to teach us to let go and let Him have control. We must relinquish control of everyone and everything around us. We can't wrestle with God for control and maintain our peace, and where there is no peace there is no joy. Ultimately, we must learn to surrender all to Jesus.

In the next seven steps, I will share with you how to experience a life of peace and joy. I also encourage you to access the companion video training I've created, "7 Steps to Experiencing a Life Filled With Peace and Joy." During this session, I will guide you through the steps.

7 STEPS to Experiencing a Life Filled With Peace and Joy

Step 1 – Cultivate Your Relationship With God

Spend quality time with God every day. Read your Bible, pray, and worship God. Cultivate your relationship *with* God rather than striving to *do* for God. Realize that your relationship with God is not based on the things that you do for Him, but upon your relationship with Him. Your doing should simply come forth from your being with Him – not vice versa.

Honor the Sabbath giving one day a week to God. It is vital to cultivating your relationship with Him. That's why it's a command and not a suggestion.

Step 2 – Take Captive Your Thoughts

One of the greatest battles you will face is the battle in your mind. Your thoughts are a driving force for your life. If your thoughts are not controlled by the Holy Spirit, you will find yourself on a path you never intended to travel.

2 Corinthians 10:5 in the Passion translation says, "We capture, like prisoners of war, every thought and insist that it bow in obedience to the Anointed One." You must go to war for your mind because that's where the battle rages.

Step 3 – Guard Your Words

Proverbs 18:21 says, "Death and life are in the power of the tongue, And those who love it and indulge it will eat its fruit and bear the consequences of their words." Matthew 12:37 says, "The words you say will either acquit you or condemn you." Words are powerful! You must be careful what you say, when you say it, and how you say it.

Step 4 – Speak God's Truths

There is power in the spoken word. Therefore, speak peace over your life. Proclaim that you are filled with the joy of the Lord. Declare His Word over your life. By doing so, you will activate the Word of God in your life. Writing down declarations can be a powerful way to instill God's truths in your heart and life. Speak all the good we can and watch your troubles wash away.

Step 5 – Choose to Experience God's Peace and Joy

Experiencing joy and peace is a CHOICE that you must make every day. You can allow the circumstances of life to weigh you down or you can choose to rise above them. It's easy to have peace and joy when things in life are going well, but you must be intentional about choosing them when times are challenging. Choose to have the Prince of Peace rule and reign over your life each and every day.

Step 6 – Receive God's Gift of Peace

As John 14:27 tells us, God left His peace when He left this world. However, you must receive this gift to achieve peace in your life. It is truly a gift, and it's not natural to receive this gift when the world is falling apart around you. However, it is available for you, and it is yours if you will receive it. You don't have to ask for it because a gift is given freely. You just have to receive it. It's that simple.

Step 7 - Keep Your Eyes on Jesus

When Peter took his eyes off of Jesus during the storm, he began to sink, and that's exactly what will happen to you if you take your eyes off Jesus. You will begin to drown when you look at everything going on around you. Jesus is reaching out his hand and asking you to come to Him. Keep your eyes fixed on Jesus, and you will walk on water!

In Hebrews 12:2, the Word of God says, "We look away from the natural realm and we focus our attention and expectation onto Jesus who birthed faith within us and who leads us forward into faith's perfection…" The focus should always be Jesus.

Final Thoughts

Hold on to Jesus, my friend. If you fall, get back up. If you feel down, keep moving forward. If you feel that you have lost your joy, purpose in your heart to find it again.

God is right there with you, and He is beckoning you to a lifetime of His peace and joy no matter what is happening in your life. Reach out your hand and take His hand. Allow God to walk with you through the storms of life.

Sit in your Father's lap a while. Lay your head on His chest. Tell Him how you feel and share your burdens with Him. Embrace your loving Heavenly Father. As you feel His loving embrace, you will feel His peace and joy envelop your life. God is truly all that you need.

A Special Invitation

The most important conversation you will ever have with God is when you ask His son, Jesus, to be Lord and Savior of your life. You may know of God, but you've never asked his son, Jesus, to reign in your heart and life. Today is the perfect day to fully commit and surrender your life to God.

It's very simple to invite Jesus into your life. Here's your 3-step process.

ADMIT that you are a sinner and need a Savior. Romans 3:23

BELIEVE that Jesus is the son of God, died on the cross, and rose again for you. John 3:16

CONFESS that Jesus is Lord of your life and commit to following Him. Romans 10:9

Congratulations on your decision and new life in Christ!

Now What?

You will want to be baptized as a profession of your faith.

Commit to regular attendance at a Bible-believing church and grow as a disciple of Christ.

"Then Jesus came to them and said, "'All authority in heaven and on earth has been given to me. [19] Therefore go and make disciples of all nations, baptizing them in the name of the Father and of the Son and of the Holy Spirit, [20] and teaching them to obey everything I have commanded you. And surely I am with you always, to the very end of the age.'" Matthew 28:18 - 20

Let me know about your decision to follow Christ by contacting me at susan@susanbelisle.com

About the Author

Susan is the Amazon best-selling author of 40 Conversations With God That Will Change Your Life. She is also the author of Healing the Hurts of Ministry: 7 Strategies for Moving Forward.

Susan resides in Roanoke, Virginia where she serves in ministry with her husband, Sam, at Celebration Church. Serving in ministry with Sam is both a privilege and an adventure that they enjoy taking together.

Susan's greatest desire is to develop leaders, build alliances, and advance God's Kingdom throughout the world. She endeavors to do this through service in the local church as well as ministering outside the walls of the church.

Susan has traveled and ministered internationally and reaches near and far through her writing and Called 2 Ministry which she founded in 2017. Its' mission is to encourage, equip, and empower women called to ministry.

Before serving in full-time ministry, Susan worked in the fields of Human Resources, Training and Development, and management. She earned a Bachelor's degree from Lee University and a Master's degree in Education and Human Development from The George Washington University. Susan is also a credentialed minister.

Outside of ministry, some of Susan's favorite pastimes include spending time with her family, having lunch with friends, drinking herbal tea, bike riding, and traveling.

Connect with Susan

It would be great to connect with you outside the pages of this book. Meet me inside the 40 Conversations with God Facebook Group for more dialogue with God and others.

www.Facebook.com/groups/40conversationswithGod

Pastors' wives, Ministers' wives, and women ministers are invited to join me in the Called 2 Ministry private Facebook group:

https://www.facebook.com/groups/1560788833975891

Visit my website for more information and resources.

www.susanbelisle.com

Susan Belisle   Susan Belisle   Susan Belisle

https://www.facebook.com/groups/314992886948619

https://www.instagram.com/susanbelisle/

https://www.youtube.com/channel/UCjvz5tKnZqrpsx-Vw8a7Y5YA

An Opportunity to Give Back

If you have been blessed by this book, would you help me share the message with others? I encourage you to purchase a copy at Amazon for a friend or family member. You will have the opportunity to help me give it away for free on Kindle every quarter, also.

You can also help me spread the word by sharing my book's advertisement from one of my social media accounts. Go to the Connect with Susan page and learn more.

Lastly, I would greatly appreciate it if you would share a thoughtful review on Amazon. It will only take a few minutes and will go a long way toward promoting my book. Just click on the link below.

Go to: www.SusanBelisle.com/review

Thank you so much for your help. I pray that the Lord blesses you as you have blessed me and others.

More Books by Susan Belisle

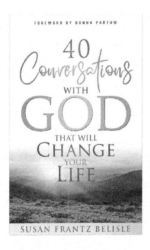

JUST ONE WORD FROM GOD CAN CHANGE EVERYTHING

Do you long to hear from God? Prayer doesn't have to be a one-way conversation. You can experience a deep and intimate relationship with God as you hear from Him about what matters most to you.

Be spending time in God's presence, guided by these daily devotions, you will:

- ✓ Feel God's comfort amid day-to-day trials
- ✓ Find hope and encouragement to face an uncertain future
- ✓ Sense God's love and tender care for you
- ✓ Get clear directions to guide your steps
- ✓ Strengthen your faith with scripture, reflection, and prayer

Hearing God's voice is not just for the super-spiritual or saints of old. He still speaks today. He is waiting for you to tune out the noise of the world and tune into His still, small voice. That's exactly what this devotional journal will help you do.

Each of the 40 Conversations with God features a scripture, spiritual reflection, prayer, and journaling space.

Healing the Hurts of Ministry: 7 Strategies for Moving Forward

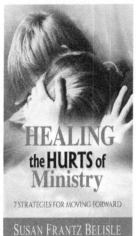

Have you been hurt by those you have served in ministry? Drawing from her experience as a Pastor's wife, Susan shares the lessons she learned and the 7 strategies she implemented for healing the hurts of ministry.

Here are just a few of the benefits of reading this eBook. You will...

- ✓ Be set free from the prison of unforgiveness
- ✓ Release emotional pain and feel the peace that forgiveness brings
- ✓ Experience intimacy with God by going deeper into His presence
- ✓ Take control of your life by unleashing the power of God's Word
- ✓ Benefit from surrounding yourself with spiritually wise mentors
- ✓ Enjoy a balanced life and feel guilt-free about taking good care of yourself
- ✓ Go from a lack of joy to an abundance of joy
- ✓ Learn how to trust God in the toughest of times

Get your free copy at: www.susanbelisle.com

Acknowledgments

Jesus Christ my Lord and Savior – I am truly amazed at how you have impacted lives through the *40 Conversations With God That Will Change Your Life* book. Thank you for giving me this second devotional to share with others. Truly, we wrote this together. I treasure our intimate conversations and am humbled that you use me to speak to others. It's always an exciting adventure as we travel together, and I can't wait to see where you take me next!

Sam Belisle – Thank you for always believing in me and supporting my God-given dreams. You continually stand by my side cheering me on and celebrating all that God is doing through my writing and in my life. Thank you for the sacrifices you have made so that I can share God's heart with others. My second book is yet another "labor of love" and you have patiently labored alongside me. God divinely brought us together knowing all that He had planned for us. There's no one else that I would rather do life and ministry with. I love you more.

Donna Partow – The lessons that I learned from you during the writing of my first book, *40 Conversations With God That Will Change Your Life*, made it possible to write this second book. Thank you for celebrating my successes, and working incredibly hard to ensure that *40 Conversations With God* became an Amazon bestseller. You continue to be a mentor and inspiration to me as I reflect upon all that I have learned from you. I am grateful that God has joined us together for His Kingdom's purposes.

40 Conversations Readers – You have been such an inspiration to me, and I am grateful for your encouragement along the way. It's been a privilege to connect with you and experience what God is doing in your lives through 40 Conversations. Thanks for taking this journey with me!

Made in the USA
Las Vegas, NV
29 November 2023

81749848R00066